D0564368

Bowie Songs:
1 Heroes
2 Life on Mars?
3 Space Oddity
4 Rebel Rebel
5 Moonage Daydream
6 Kooks
7 Suffragette City
8 Golden Years
9 Starman
10 Ashes to Ashes

MORE FUN THINGS TO DO:
- MAKE HALLOWEEN COSTUMES
- DRAW BATS
- Eat MARSHMALLOWS
- BANG POTS AND PANS
- SWING ON SOMETHING
- DRAW MORE BATS

Small Winged Insects:
- Sphinx Moth
- Lady Butterfly
- American Bumblebee
- Tiger Moth
- Big Dipper Firefly
- Blue Winged Wasp
- Milkweed Bug
- Zebra Butterfly
- Paper Wasp
- Cucumber Beetle

Ghastly Illnesses:
Moon Blindness
Teen Flu
Lethargitis
Purple Sky Virus
The Great Cough
Hopping Complex
Hectic Exam Fever
Worrygroit
Cauliflower Tongue
Unicornitis
The Sweet Plague

Shades of Black:
1. Midnight
2. Charcoal
3. Jet
4. Licorice
5. Ebony
6. Onyx
7. Outer Space
8. Café Noir
9. Bike Grease
10. Raven

Fearsome Enemies:
- Toto
- Lanie
- Snoopy
- Snowy

For Tara Walker.
With thanks to Júlia Sardà and Scott Richardson—K.M.

For Carmela. Welcome—J.S.

Tundra Books, a division of Random House of Canada Limited, a Penguin Random House Company

LIBRARY AND ARCHIVES CANADA CATALOGUING IN PUBLICATION

Maclear, Kyo, 1970-, author
The Liszts / by Kyo Maclear ; illustrated by Júlia Sardà.
Issued in print and electronic formats.
ISBN 978-1-77049-496-1 (bound).—ISBN 978-1-77049-497-8 (epub)

I. Sardà, Júlia, 1987-, illustrator II. Title.
PS8625.L435L59 2016 JC813'.6 C2015-905755-8 C2015-905756-6

Published simultaneously in the United States of America by Tundra Books of Northern New York, a division of Random House of Canada Limited, a Penguin Random House Company

LIBRARY OF CONGRESS CONTROL NUMBER: 2015954162

Edited by Tara Walker
Designed by Júlia Sardà with assistance from CS Richardson
The artwork in this book was rendered digitally.
Handlettering by Júlia Sardà.

PRINTED AND BOUND IN CHINA

www.penguinrandomhouse.ca

1 2 3 4 5 20 19 18 17 16

THE LISZTS

written by

KYO MACLEAR

illustrated by

JÚLIA SARDÀ

TUNDRA BOOKS

The Liszts made lists.
Scritch, scratch.
They made lists most usual.

And lists most unusual.

Mama made lists of ghastly illnesses
and the greatest soccer players of all time.

Papa made lists of dreaded chores
and small winged insects.

They made lists in winter, spring, summer, fall.

They made lists every day except Sundays,
which were listless.

Their lists filled the house.

Scritch, scratch.

Frederick, the youngest child, made lists of fun things to do.

Winifred, the oldest child, preferred her top ten lists.

Edward, the middle child, made lists that went on for 31 pages. Lists to quiet the swirl of his midnight mind.
MOBY DICK

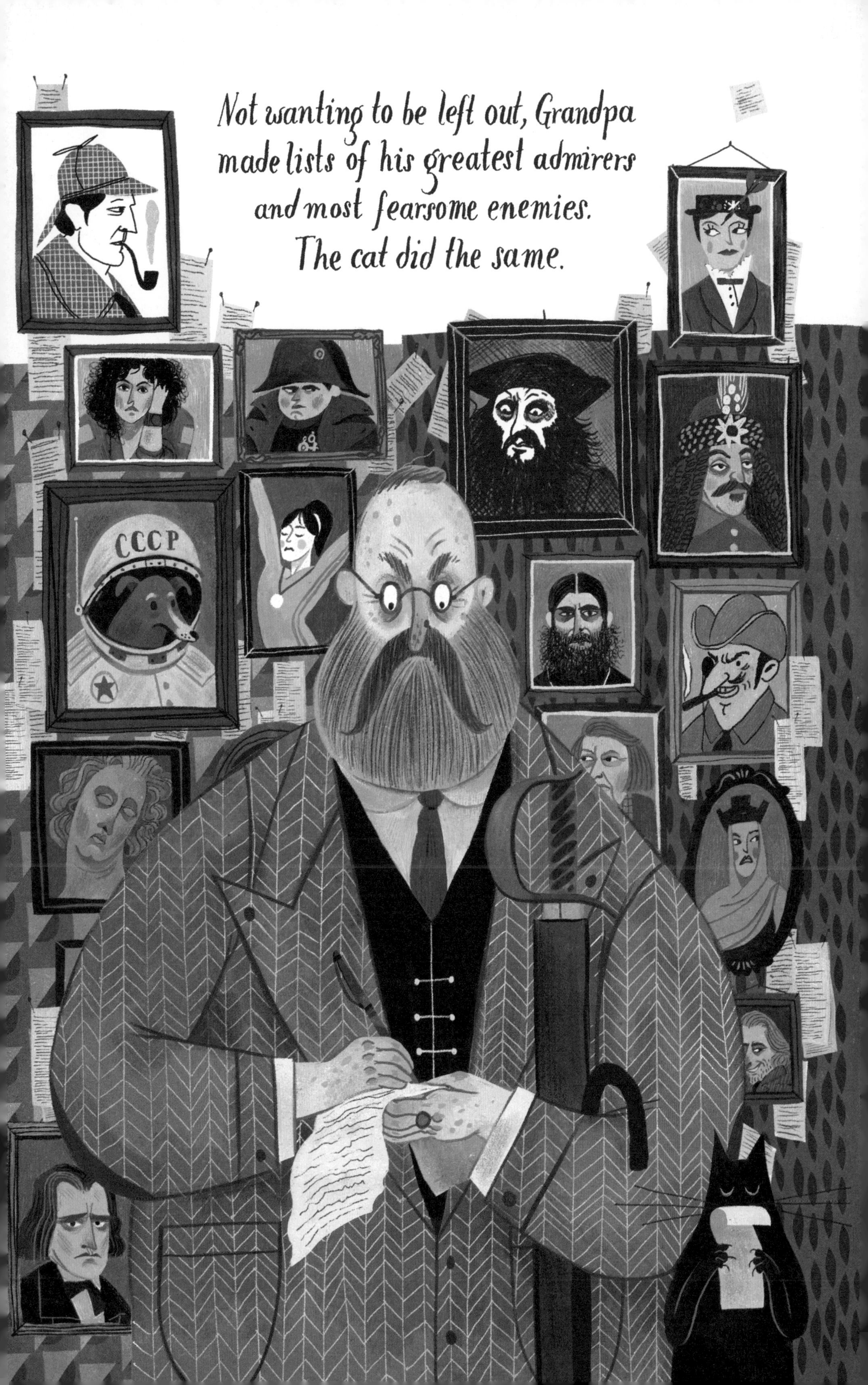
Not wanting to be left out, Grandpa made lists of his greatest admirers and most fearsome enemies. The cat did the same.
CCCP

The lists grew and multiplied.

Then one day
a visitor arrived.
His feet were tired.
The door was open.

"I'm here," he said to Mama.
"Are you on the list?" she asked.
"No", he said.
"You're not Pelé?"
"No."
"Ronaldo?"
"No."
"Then I'm sorry," she said,
getting back to her list.

"I'm here," the visitor said
to Papa, who said:
"Are you here
about the hedges?"
"No."
"Are you here to fix the roof?"
"No."
"Are you on the list?"
"No."
"Then I'm sorry," he said.

The visitor went to see Grandpa, who said:
"Are you Mr. Paws, the dreadful dungeon dragon?"
"No."
"Are you Sally Mae, the lovely acrobat?"
"No."
"Well then. I'm sorry."

"I'm here," he said to Frederick, the youngest one, who said: "Did you bring the black Lego? Are you a Horseman of the Apocalypse? Are you squishy?"

"No, no, no," said the visitor. "But I thought... the door was open. Oh never mind."

The visitor watered the flowers
and fixed the roof.
He trimmed the hedges.

"I'm here," he said to the cat,
who said nothing.
"I'm here," he said to Winifred,
the oldest one, who just said:
"Are you a hairstylist?"

The visitor tidied and decorated.
He trimmed his hair.
He had a long nap...

When he awoke he noticed Edward,
the middle one, looking a bit lost,
with nothing but a list of questions.

He had a good feeling about this one.

"I'm here," he said, and Edward said: "Hi."
"The door was open."
"I know. I left the door open."
"You did?"
"Yes."
"For me?"
"I think so."

At first they were a bit shy.

But then Edward discovered
that the visitor had questions too.
Lots of them.

-WHERE DO WE
COME FROM?
-HOW DO I KNOW
MY LIFE IS NOT
A DREAM?

- DO COLORS LOOK THE SAME FOR EVERYONE?
- WHERE ARE MY PANTS?
- IF MY ARMS WERE STRONGER, COULD I PICK MYSELF UP?
- WHERE DO THE THINGS WE FORGET GO?
- WHERE DID I PARK THE CAR?

So Edward felt free to ask his own:

- DOES ANYONE OWN THE MOON OR THE SKY?
- WHERE DO MY THOUGHTS COME FROM?
- WHAT ABOUT MY BAD DREAMS?
- *WHY AM I RIGHT-HANDED?*
- WHY DO I HAVE TWO EYES IF I ONLY SEE ONE THING?
- WHERE DID INFINITY START AND HOW WILL IT END?

"Want to do something?" asked the visitor.
"Sure," said Edward.
"What should we do?"
"I don't know. Why don't we just start something and see what happens?"

The visitor stayed for dinner.
And breakfast.
And lunch.
And tea.
And dinner.
And breakfast.
And, well, forever.

The Liszts Kept making lists. Scritch, scratch.

They made lists most usual. And lists most unusual.

But now they always left a space at the bottom.
"Just in case," said Edward,
"something unexpected comes up."